Mr Crookodile

For Robert, Bonnie and Kimara - J.B.
For Ella - K.P.

First published in Great Britain 2006
by Egmont UK Ltd
239 Kensington High Street, London W8 6SA
Text copyright © John Bush 2006
Illustrations copyright © Korky Paul 2006
The author and illustrator have asserted their moral rights
ISBN 978 1 4052 2229 7
ISBN 1 4052 2229 8
10 9 8 7 6 5 4 3 2 1
A CIP catalogue record for this title is available from the British Library.
Printed in Singapore.

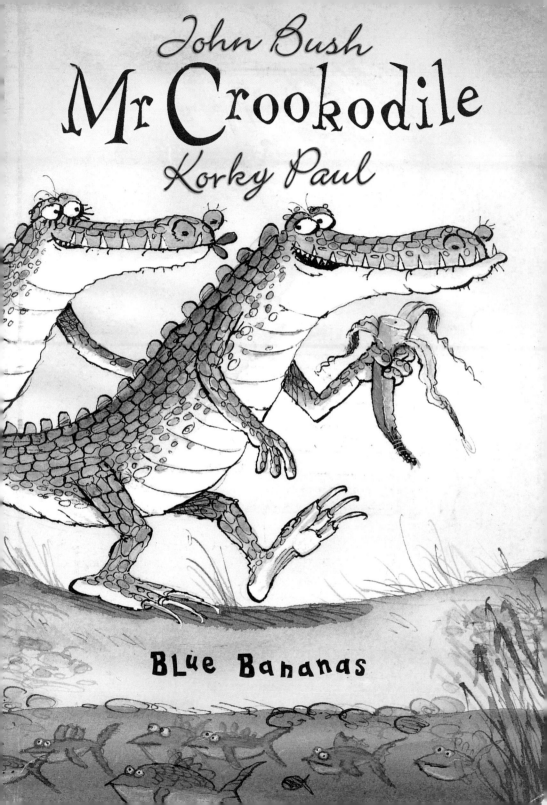

John Bush

Mr Crookodile

Korky Paul

BLue Bananas

It was eight o'clock in the evening.

In the Crocodile riverbank home,

supper was over and the children were

tucked up in bed, fast asleep.

Mr Crocodile was about to settle back in his favourite chair and watch TV when Mrs Crocodile called out from the kitchen, 'Let's do the dishes, dear.'

Mr Crocodile knew this meant just one thing. He was in for a good talking to.

'I've been thinking,' Mrs Crocodile began as Mr Crocodile started on the dishes. 'I'm sick and tired of living in this dank, dark, smelly hole in the riverbank.'

'But this is how crocodiles live, dear!'

Mr Crocodile exclaimed. 'I thought

we were happy!'

I'm happy with our life.

'Well, I am not. All you do is float around on your belly all day trying to look like a log so you can catch poor, helpless, harmless animals.'

You're a lazy animal trap!

'But that's what crocodiles do, dear!' cried Mr Crocodile, all hurt and in a huff. 'It's not as if we're vegetarians!'

'There must be something more useful you could do,' Mrs Crocodile continued.

'Perhaps if you became a vegetarian you'd have the time to get yourself a respectable job so we can live a little better and give our children a decent education.'

Mr Crocodile dropped the bowl he was washing in dismay at the thought of becoming a vegetarian and having to work for a living.

Xeccchh!

'Here, let me finish those dishes before you break any more,' said Mrs Crocodile, shooing him out of the kitchen.

'If you can't think of something, *I'll* go out and get a job and *you* can do the housework,' she called after him.

'I couldn't bear the thought of your having to do that, my love,' he called back in alarm. 'Never you mind. A job I shall find.'

I hate work!

Mr Crocodile went to the bedroom to
think. Somehow he could always
think better lying down.

'If I'm going to have to work for a living, I might as well make it really worth my while,' he thought out loud. 'Let's see, who makes pots of money these days?'

And then it struck him.

'Got it!' he cried. 'Soccer stars make

a mint. I can see it all. Mr Soccerdile!

The fame, the fans, the fortune!'

'The punctured soccer balls,' added
Mrs Crocodile, bringing him a mug
of cocoa. 'No soccer ball could
survive a kick from a foot with those
dreadful toenails.'

17

'Hmmmph, didn't think of that,' Mr

Crocodile muttered.

'Well, who else makes loads of

money? I know!' he whooped.

'Pop stars are fabulously rich. I can see it all. Mr Rockodile! The fun, the fast life, the fortune! The whole world's going to rock around this croc!'

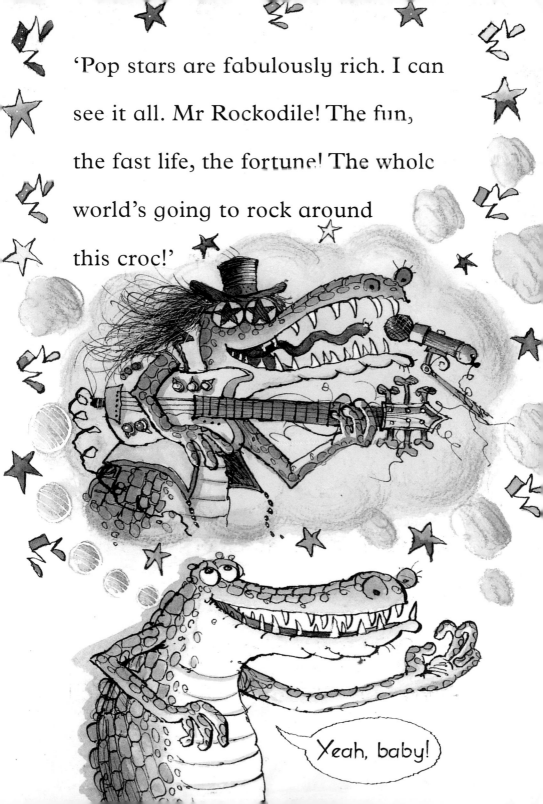

Yeah, baby!

'I think not, dear,' said Mrs

Crocodile. 'When you sing in the

bath the children start crying!'

'Hmmmph, didn't think of that

either,' he sighed.

'Well, how about Mr Cookodile?' he cried, as a brilliant new thought flashed to mind. 'I can see it all! Let's open a restaurant called Mr Croc's Pot and rake in the money.'

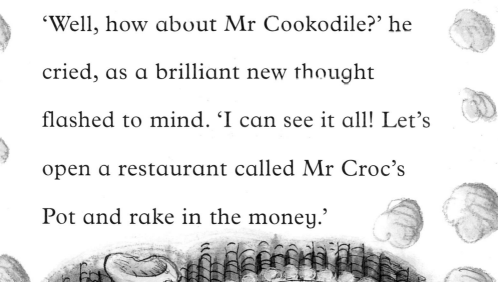

'Now, that's a fine idea,' said his wife,

excitedly. 'But you can't make toast

without burning it, so I'll do the cooking

and you can do the washing up.'

Delicious plan!

'Not if I can help it,' mumbled

Mr Crocodile under his breath,

as his wife left the bedroom to fetch

her recipe books.

And then he had the brightest

thought of all. 'Not Mr Cookodile!

Mr Crookodile

'I'm going to rob the Baboon Bush Bank tomorrow and help myself to all their money. I'm big. I'm terrifying. I'm a natural. I can see it now. Loads and loads of lovely loot!

'But wait a minute. I'm also easily recognisable. I'd better start thinking about a good disguise.

'Give me your loot or I'll rip your head off!' he roared, rehearsing out loud.

'Pardon, dear?' said Mrs Crocodile,

returning with her recipe books.

'Nothing, my love,' he replied sweetly.

'Just practising. I've decided to go for

a job interview at the bank tomorrow.

I don't think a restaurant's such a

good idea after all.

'You would have to work far too hard. Let's sleep on it and see what tomorrow brings. Nighty-night,' he whispered as he blew out the candle.

The next morning, the moment his
wife left to walk the children to
school, Mr Crocodile began to put on
his disguise.

They'll never know it's me!

He put on his longest overcoat.

He tied his children's tennis racquets

to his feet to hide his footprints.

He pulled a large bush hat down on his head.

As a finishing touch he took his son's fake glasses, with a false nose and moustache, and stuck them to his face with candle wax.

'Who would know that beneath this cunning disguise lurks the greatest bank robber of all time?' he laughed, admiring himself in the mirror.

'Give me your loot or I'll rip your head off!' he rehearsed one last time. Then he set off to rob the bank.

He began imagining himself

swimming in a river of money, when

the tennis racquets on his feet broke.

'Bah!' he groaned. 'Too bad.'

'When I'm rich I will build my very own tennis court and buy all the racquets I need. For now, I'd better walk on my heels to hide my footprints.'

My feet are killing me!

He started clumsily hobbling along
on his heels. Suddenly a gust of wind
whipped off his hat and blew it into a
tree, way out of Mr Crocodile's reach.

'I never liked that smelly old hat anyway,' he muttered. 'When I have mounds of money, I'll buy a new hat for every day of the year. At least I still have my fake glasses, nose and moustache.'

Minutes later, the sun melted the wax
that secured them and they fell off.

'A good crook never quits,' he said,

drawing himself into his great big

coat so no one could see who was

inside.

Mr Crocodile hobbled on, determined as ever. At last, peering through the second buttonhole in his coat, he could see the Baboon Bush Bank ahead.

I smell money!

But as he got closer, a large

thorn-bush snagged his coat and

ripped it right off.

'Mr Crocodile!' the passers-by cried.

'What on earth are you doing out of

the water?'

Um...

Mr Crocodile wasn't lying down so he couldn't think of a good, quick answer. 'I . . . er . . . I . . . um . . . I'm . . . mmm . . . I'm not sure,' he stammered.

At that very moment a huge commotion broke out inside the bank. The Howling Hyena Gang burst out, carrying bags full of money.

'They're stealing my money!' Mr Crocodile panicked.

'Oh no you don't!' he growled as the

gang ran past.

Three swipes of his mighty tail and they were all laid out flat.

Mr Crocodile leaped on top of them
and snatched up the bags of money.

However, before Mr Crocodile could escape, he found himself completely surrounded by a cheering throng.

Next thing, the Bank Manager was

patting him heartily on the back.

'Mr Crocodile,' he said, 'you are just

the man I've been looking for.

I'm offering you a position in our

bank as Chief of Security.

Please, please say you accept.'

Mr Crocodile took the position, delighted that there was, after all, an honest job he could do to earn good money.

The family moved to a comfortable
new home near the Baboon Bush
Bank, which, thanks to Mr Crocodile,
never had a single attempt at another
robbery.

They all became vegetarians too,
much to Mr Crocodile's disgust.

And from that day on, the only sneaky thing that Mr Crocodile ever did was slink into the bakery to buy an occasional, yummy tiger fish and mopani worm pie.

Only when Mrs Crocodile wasn't looking, of course.